This book belongs to

Paul Dudonis Jr.

Walt Disney®

VOLUME 10

SIMPLE SCIENCE

WALT DISNEY FUN-TO-LEARN LIBRARY

A BANTAM BOOK

NEW YORK · TORONTO · LONDON · SYDNEY · AUCKLAND

ISBN 0-553-05514-3

Published simultaneously in the United States and Canada. Bantam Books are published by Bantam Books, Inc. Its trademark, consisting of the words "Bantam Books" and the portrayal of a rooster, is Registered in U.S. Patent and Trademark Office and in other countries. Marca Registrada. Bantam Books, Inc., 666 Fifth Avenue, New York, New York 10103. Printed in the United States of America. 19   18   17   16   15   14   13   12   11   10

Classic® binding, R. R. Donnelley & Sons Company. U.S. Patent No. 4,408,780; Patented in Canada 1984; Patents in other countries issued or pending.

Do you like mysteries? Isn't it exciting when you solve one? The world is full of mysteries. Do you know how sounds are made? Do you know how plants grow?

Mickey and his friends are always asking questions like these and trying to find the answers. That's how they learn about science. And it's a good way to have fun.

You already have the most important things you need to be a science detective — your eyes, ears, hands, mouth, and nose. They'll help you see, hear, touch, taste, and smell the things around you. Mickey and his friends love to solve mysteries. They are looking for clues. Are you ready to look for some, too?

There are all kinds of clues to tell you what is going on around you. Sounds can tell you a lot of things. A ringing alarm clock tells you it's time to get up. A clap of thunder tells you it's time to go inside before you get caught in a storm. Sometimes you don't even notice how special a sound can be. That's why Morty and Ferdie are playing a game called "name that sound." It's Ferdie's turn to guess.

The house where Morty and Ferdie live is full of different sounds. Can you hear some of the same sounds in your house? And what are some of the sounds you hear when you go outside? How many can *you* name?

"Here's another special kind of sound," says Mickey. "You can make your own music!"

He puts a rubber band around a cake pan and pulls it. *Plink!* Then he pulls harder. *PLINK!* The rubber band moves faster and the sound gets louder. Mickey puts another rubber band around the pan. It's Mickey's one-man cake pan band!

"I'll show you how to make a kazoo," says Minnie, joining in the fun.

She takes the cardboard tube from a roll of toilet paper and covers one end with wax paper.

Then she puts a rubber band around the wax paper to hold it tight.

She uses a pencil to poke a small hole in the tube, near the wax paper.

"How do you play it?" asks Morty. Minnie puts the open end of the kazoo in her mouth and hums a tune.

Now it's the Mickey Mouse marching band. Why don't you join in?

"But how does sound travel from one place to another so you can hear it?" asks Morty.

"I'll show you how to make a string telephone," says Mickey. "Then you can see for yourselves. Morty, you get a long piece of string, and Ferdie can get two paper cups."

Mickey uses a pencil to poke a small hole in the bottom of each paper cup. Ferdie puts one end of the string through each hole. Morty ties a knot in each end of the string so it won't pull back through the hole. Then they stretch the string tight and make sure it isn't touching anything.

"What's new!" Morty shouts into one end as Ferdie listens.

"We just made a telephone," Ferdie answers.

"I can see the string moving up and down as you talk," says Morty.
"Let's pretend we're calling one another from different spaceships."

Can you think of some things that make their own light? Peter, Wendy, Michael, and John are camping in the woods of Never Land. They have plenty of supplies with them, including some things to help them see in the dark. During the day, the sun gave them all the light they needed, but by nightfall, they're glad they have a campfire, candles, a flashlight, a lantern—and Tinker Bell, of course!

Wendy is showing John how night and day happen. First she sticks a leaf on one side of an orange. "That's Never Land," she says.

Then she holds the orange up in the air and pretends it's Earth.

John shines his flashlight at the orange. As Wendy slowly turns the orange, the leaf is sometimes on the dark side, and sometimes in the light.

"I get it, Wendy," says John. "My flashlight is just like the sun!"

When the sun is shining on our part of Earth, it's day. And when our part of Earth turns away from the sun, it's night. As Earth turns, we have day and night.

"I can do anything," says Peter.
"I can even make a rainbow.
Watch this!"

He fills a clear plastic glass with water almost to the top.
He puts the glass on the edge of a tree stump
in the sunlight. He makes sure the glass
is partly on and partly off the tree stump, so
that the sun will shine right through it.

Then he puts a piece of paper on the ground near the tree stump.

Peter moves the paper until the sunlight passes through the water and shines right on the paper.

"It *is* a rainbow," cries Michael.

"I told you so," says Peter.

Light is made up of many different colors. When light shines through water, you can see them all.

How many colors do you see? Wendy's favorite color is blue. Do you like one color best of all?

Peter thinks he's being followed, because every time he turns around he sees someone behind him. Do you know who it is?
It's his shadow!

Can you find your shadow, too? Look for your shadow on a sunny day and then on a cloudy day. Does your shadow look the same on both days?

Light can shine through water, but it can't shine through you. When you stand in the sun, you block the light. That dark space that the light can't reach is your shadow.

Peter, Wendy, John, and Michael are making a shadow puppet play. They shine a light on a white wall and hold up their fingers in front of the light. Some shapes they make look like animals, others look like people.

"Mine's a monster," says Michael.

"Mine's a rabbit," says Wendy.

"Mine's the best," says Peter. "It can fly, just like me."

Where is the place in your house that has the best tastes and smells? Huey, Dewey, and Louie love to help in the kitchen at Grandma Duck's house. On baking day, there are lots of things to smell and taste.

It's Huey's job to beat the egg whites. "Yuk," says Louie, staring at the slippery mixture. When the egg whites are beaten, he takes a taste. "Now they look different," he says, "but they still don't taste very good."

BLESS OUR FARM

"Just wait until the cake is finished," says Grandma. It's Dewey's job to stir in the sugar. Louie and Huey add the rest of the ingredients.

They all take turns mixing until the batter is smooth. Louie licks some batter off his finger. "It's delicious!" he exclaims.

Finally, Grandma pops the cake in the oven. As it bakes, the kitchen fills up with wonderful smells. What started as a little of this and a little of that comes out—completely different!

But wait! Suppose Dewey had used salt instead of sugar when he helped mix up the cake. Let's see what happens when you make a mistake.

Oh, Dewey! Salt and sugar may look the same, but they taste very different. If you use the wrong one, you'll know for sure by the way the cake tastes. Do you think Grandma's homemade ice cream would take away some of that nasty taste?

Huey, Dewey, and Louie are playing a taste game. They have gathered peanuts, raisins, popcorn, lemon slices, and some other surprises and put them separately into paper cups. Each kind of food has its own special taste.

It's Louie's turn to close his eyes and try to guess what food is in his cup.

"It's sour, salty, crunchy, and juicy," cries Louie.

What do you think it is?

"I have a riddle for you, Pooh," says Christopher Robin. "What's inside the honey jar when there's no honey left?"

"My nose," says Pooh, "I'm always looking for the last drop."

"Silly bear," says Christopher Robin, kindly, "When you've eaten all the honey, the jar is full of air. You can't see air. But air is all around you —above you, behind you, and on either side, too."

"You can't eat air for lunch," grumbles Pooh.

Air is what's inside a balloon when you blow it up.

Air is what comes out of a balloon when you let it go.

Air is what's inside a bubble.

And when you blow through a straw into a glass of juice, what do you think makes the bubbles?
"Air, of course, you silly Tigger," says Pooh.

"Here's another trick you can play with air," says Christopher Robin.

"I'll write you a message on a piece of paper. You crumble it up and put it at the bottom of a plastic glass. Turn the glass over so it is upside down. Then put the glass straight down into a bowl of water."

"But the paper will get wet," says Pooh.

"Just try it," says Christopher Robin.

"My goodness," says Pooh. "The paper is still dry!"

Christopher Robin reads this message, "To find the honey, do the trick again."

Christopher Robin puts another note in
the glass. But this time he tilts the glass after
he has put it in the water. When he pulls out the
message, the paper is all wet, and the ink is smeared.

"Oh, bother," says Pooh. "What went wrong?"
"Did you see those bubbles escaping from the glass?"
asked Christopher Robin. "When those air bubbles bubbled,
some water took their place. That's how the paper got
wet. But don't worry, Pooh. Just follow me. I'll show
you where the honey is."

What do you like to do on a rainy day? Today, Huey, Dewey, and Louie have put on their slickers and gone outside to play, even though it's raining. Uncle Donald takes them out to their favorite pond in the woods.

"Look at that leaf floating in the pond. It looks like a little boat," says Huey.

Dewey throws a branch in the water. "This one's an ocean liner," he says.

Donald's pine cone floats, too. They decide that one must be a tugboat. Then Huey throws a rock into the water. "What do you think of my boat?" he asks.

"That can't be a boat because it isn't floating," says Louie.

"Well..." says Huey. "Maybe it's a submarine."

It's fun to see what floats and what sinks. When Donald and the boys get back home, they try the game again, using a tub of water. You can do this yourself. Try putting a pencil, a cork, a penny, an eraser, a metal spoon, a scrap of cloth, an empty tin can, and a crumpled-up piece of paper in a large pail or a deep bowl of water. Then see what happens. Do the heavy things float and the light things sink? Or is it the other way around? Do some things float at first and then sink after a while?

Now that the rain has stopped,
the boys are out in the garden,
splashing through all the puddles.
Donald has an idea.

"Let's see what happens to Dewey's favorite puddle," he
says. He takes a stick and draws a line around the outside
of the puddle.
    Later, Dewey comes back to inspect the puddle.
    Do you know what happened? The sun was so hot, it
dried up the puddle, just as it dries your wet
bathing suit after a swim.

Do you know what happens to water when it becomes very cold?
Huey, Dewey, and Louie discover the answer when Donald shows them
how to make frozen lollipops.

He pours fruit juice into an ice-cube tray. He fills the tray almost,
but not quite, to the top.

He covers the tray with two layers of tinfoil, folded all around the
edges so it stays in place.

The boys help him push ice-cream sticks through the foil and into the center of each section of the ice-cube tray.

Then they put the tray into the freezer and leave it all night.

The next morning, after breakfast, Donald takes the ice-cube tray out of the freezer. Now the fruit juice and water has hardened into yummy frozen lollipops, just the way water in a pond or a puddle becomes frozen when the weather is very cold.

Mmm, good!

"Goofy, what picks up paper clips and safety pins, but not crayons or peanuts?"

"I know, Mickey, Clarabelle Cow's vacuum cleaner!"

"No, Goofy! It's a magnet! Here, you try."

Mickey bought his magnet at a hardware store. Any shape will do.

Hold your magnet several inches away from a paper clip.
Slowly move it closer until...*SNAP!* The paper clip jumps over to
the magnet.

Lift the magnet up. What does the paper clip do now?
"Just like magic," says Goofy.

It's fun to see what things you can pick up with a magnet. Goofy tries a plastic cup, a pencil, a bottle cap, an eraser, a house key, and a safety pin.

The plastic cup doesn't move. But what is the safety pin doing? Do you know why? A magnet will pick up something made of iron or steel, but not something made of wood or plastic.

Do you think Goofy's magnet will pick up Mickey's peanut butter-and-jelly sandwich?

Now look at what Goofy's doing. He's found a way to use his magnet as a fishing pole.
First, he makes some fish by cutting them out of colored paper.

He draws eyes with a crayon and uses a paper clip for a mouth.

Then, he ties one end of a string to a stick and ties the other end to his magnet to make a fishing pole. See how many fish he can catch!

A magnet is so strong it will still work when something gets in its way, like a piece of paper

—or like water. Mickey and Goofy are going to make a special sailboat that sails with a magnet. Here's what they need:

paper

thumbtacks

cork

pie plate

pin

shoe boxes

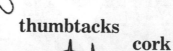

Goofy puts some thumbtacks into the bottom of a cork.

Mickey makes a paper sail with a piece of paper. He uses a pin to put the sail in the cork.

Then he puts a pie plate on two shoe boxes, leaving enough space between the boxes to fit his hand.

Mickey puts the cork boat in the water.

By moving a magnet under the plate, he sails the boat!

How does a tiny seed grow into a juicy vegetable? Spring is a fine time to find out. That's just what Mickey, Minnie, Morty, and Ferdie are doing now. They're planting their garden.

They pick out a nice sunny spot. Mickey digs the soil. Minnie rakes the soil into long, neat rows.

Morty drops seeds into the ground.

Ferdie pulls out the weeds so the little plants will have the garden to themselves.

On the days when it doesn't rain, Minnie waters the garden so the plants will have enough water to drink.

Can you see what has happened? Those tiny seeds have grown into radishes, peas, string beans, and lettuce.

"It's suppertime," says Minnie.

What happens to a seed when you put it in the ground? Pretend you have a magic looking glass that can see underground. First, you would see the tiny seed grow a root that pushes deep into the ground. A root works like a straw so the plant can drink up water and other things from the soil. Then, the seed grows a stem that shoots up, looking for light.

"Let's grow a seed indoors," Minnie says, "so we can watch it grow."
She soaks some dried beans overnight.

She wets paper towels and pushes them into a glass jar.

Then she puts the beans
between the paper and the glass.

She puts the jar by a
window where it will get
warmth and light. Every day,
she sprinkles a little water into
the jar to make sure the paper
towels stay wet.

See what's happened to
Minnie's beans!

"Don't throw away that carrot top," says Minnie one day, when she sees Ferdie munching on a juicy carrot. "I'll show you how to make a surprise for Mickey."

The boys take cut-off carrot tops and put each one in a dish lined with pebbles.

They add just enough water to cover the bottom of the carrot.

Then they hide the dishes in a place where there's not too much sun.

In just a few days, the carrot tops begin sprouting into beautiful feathery plants.

Finally, the surprises are ready. Morty and Ferdie greet Mickey at the front door.

"These are for you, Uncle Mickey," says Morty. "We grew them ourselves."

Mickey chuckles and opens a big box. He hands his nephews each a magnifying glass and a special hat.

"Here, boys," he says. "These are for my two favorite science detectives."